SHAKESPEARE IN COSMOS

SHAKESPEARE IN COSMOS

DEJAN STOJANOVIĆ

Translated by
Petra Grujin

New Avenue Books
&

ALBATROS PLUS

SHAKESPEARE IN COSMOS

English translation Copyright © 2024 New Avenue Books.

This book was originally published in Serbia in 2017 by UKS (The Association of Writers of Serbia), Belgrade, as a second part of the first book (*Ozar*) of the pentalogy *The World in Nowhereness* (Serbian: *Svet u nigdini* and a subtitle Pentalogija: *Ozar, Svet i Bog, Svet u nigdini, Svet i ljudi, Dom svetlosti*).

New Avenue Books
&
Albatros Plus

First Edition in English

Library of Congress Control Number: 2024949637

ISBN-13: 979-8-9916352-5-7

THEY SAID ABOUT *THE WORLD IN NOWHERENESS*

"When I got my hands on Dejan Stojanović's book *The World in Nowhereness*, I was amazed and read the book with great pleasure. I did not even believe there was someone today who could write such a long poem, an epic, as if I opened to read the *Iliad* in our time. I recommend this book to all believers in poetry because faith in poetry is the same as faith in eternity and eternal life."

— *Matija Bećković*

"*The World in Nowhereness* is Dejan Stojanović's utopian absolute book, a Mallarméan absolute. An absolute story, or an absolute book, according to Borges, is a desert-like book: sandy, grainily unforeseeable, and corpuscularly innumerable. It is simultaneously a vision and a chimera. Isn't that precisely why we long for an absolute book? *The World in Nowhereness* by Dejan Stojanović is, in his way, an embodiment of that dream."

— *Srba Ignjatović*

"I have always wondered, even about my poetic work, what a total poem is… Can the pentalogy by Dejan Stojanović be called a total poem that every poet of note has dreamed about since Homer? I felt such impulses while reading *The World in Nowhereness*. This is an absolute poem, of an absolute system of thought that reaches across the totality of our civilizational legacies."

— *Duško Novaković*

"Exactly 17 years ago, in the last year of the 20th century, I came across the work of Dejan Stojanović, and then I wrote a text from which I will extract a few sentences. "Dejan Stojanović, in the last two years, made a real feat; he published six books, except for one, all books of poetry." This first five-book collection was published in the last year of the 20th century, and here we are now with the five-book collection in the XXI century, nearing the end of the second decade. And then I also wrote the following: "Stojanović is a poet who searches for the perfect poetic form because at the same time he searches for the absolute meaning of human existence." Whether it was a hunch or not, there is the Pentalogy, and there is that word, that concept – an absolute, an absolute book, an absolute poem that could be sensed even in that first pentalogy, in those poems that he published at that time."

— *Aleksandar Petrov* (January 17, 2018)

"(*The World in Nowhereness* offers) the joy of cognition due to discoveries worthy of the Nobel Prize…"

— *Milan Lukić*

"*The World in Nowhereness* is primarily the result of great literary ambition and faith in literature. It was not only Kiš who said that literature is created by form and that Sartre's quote should be placed at the entrance to the Association of Serbian Writers that "someone does not become a writer to say certain things, but to say them in a certain way." Dejan Stojanović is one of those who think well about that way and think very sovereignly and broadly. Even in how he approaches the form, we can see the breadth of his education, including the humanities and the natural sciences. However, perhaps more than anything else, he enters into some area of spirituality and, I would even dare say, esoteric. If you read Dejan Stojanović, your life will not be the same – it will be better."

— *Muharem Bazdulj*

"It has been quite a while since we had, if at all, a poetic pentalogy in Serbian poetry."

— *Dušan Stojković*

Dejan Stojanović's poetic-philosophical book *The World in Nowhereness*, both in form and content, is an original and exceptional literary work and can be considered a rare literary event in Serbian poetry and on the world stage.

— *Nevena Vitošević*

"It is every poet's dream to write a relevant, unique, comprehensive book in which he will properly present all his thoughts and feelings that have appeared in his long conversations with the world. By the *world,* I mean everything manifested and abstract in (a) language, what is named, and what can be named. Dejan Stojanović's extensive pentalogy *The World in Nowhereness* is an attempt at writing such a book. This pentalogy about the world and light is an ambitious endeavor."

— Bratislav R. Milanović

"*The World in Nowhereness*, the pentalogy by Dejan Stojanović, is an unusual endeavor in Serbian literature."

— Nikola Marinković

"*The World in Nowhereness*, a poetic endeavor by Dejan Stojanović, is an exceptional occurrence in Serbian."

— Dragan Kolarević

"There are very few such books in Serbian literature."

— Ivan Cvetanović

"(The publishing of *The World in Nowhereness* is) a significant date in contemporary Serbian poetry."

— Miljurko Vukadinović

"Steadfast and consistent, with his mapping out of circular trajectories in the realms of poetry and philosophy, and always being something more than the sum of all parts, Dejan Stojanović has proved to be a thinker of continuously inventive thought. He belongs to that creative ilk whose body of work affirms the permanence of the long-established unity of the Mystic and the Magus. On the one hand, he is one of those with extensive knowledge and who, according to Bela Hamvash, are Mystics. Yet, he is also one of the Magi, who also possesses knowledge, but one meant to encourage and reflect the urge to peer into the other, lesser-known or completely unexplored side, which light cannot reach at first glance."

— David Kecman Dako

Dejan Stojanović, a sincere devotee of both poetry and philosophy, achieved a real poetic feat in 2017 by publishing an extensive five-volume book titled *The World in Nowhereness*.

— Aleksandar B. Laković

"The author is deeply immersed in his attempt to decode the essence of the Universe, the meaning of the origin, and the persistence of being therein. He seeks balance and the possibility of introducing harmony into seemingly incompatible, disharmonious phenomena and concepts."

— *Gordana Vlahović*

"Dejan Stojanović offers us *The World in Nowhereness*, his latest book, as a spiritual anthology. This is an ambitious poetic and essayistic project in a predominantly philosophical, dense, and layered pentalogy about humanity as the source and the final destination of all visible and invisible worlds. The manuscript is presented in innovative, avant-garde form. Dejan Stojanović wisely and expertly intertwines poetry and prose, the epic and the lyrical, and the theoretical-critical."

— *Zorica Arsić Mandarić*

"Stojanović's pronounced contemplativeness is what makes him stand out in the contemporary world of the poetic invention as one of the few being in no quandary about the equality of poetry and philosophy and the necessity of their proper understanding, as well as a deeper decoding of the meaning behind words. For that reason, I see his search in the book *The World in Nowhereness* as a quest for the meaning of elemental survival in a time that is alienated, brutally real, and preoccupied with everything and nothing."

— *Vidak Maslovarić*

"Stojanović's poetic, prosaic, and dramatic approach represents, in a unique sense, an array of basic concepts and elements of human existence, its earthly and cosmic destiny. He tackles the subjects of freedom, the Absolute, God, the Devil, chaos, order, truth, the world, etc. The philosophical, the religious, and the poetic make up the basic core in the interpretation and understanding of the ontology of human survival."

— *Jovo Cvjetković*

Contents

SHAKESPEARE IN COSMOS

To Victoria

DEJAN STOJANOVIĆ

THE FIRST ENCOUNTER WITH HIGHER BEINGS

I find myself in a world that enables me to see everything in a better way but in which nothing seems to have its physical form. Inebriated by the beauty of many colors and shades I haven't seen so far, I am landing on the surface of an unfamiliar planet, which I can clearly see. I am starting to realize that the truth isn't always what it seems because our beliefs and concepts lose value in this new world. Thought is everything. An idea makes the basis of reality. Our ideas now look like the schemes of some captivated creatures.

A SONNET WREATH

1

On the spaceship, I'll now gladly embark
On a journey to where no one will glean
Neither who I am nor what star does spark
O'er the sky from which I come in a dream.
Nobody there has ever heard of me,
On other planets, midst their many tribes,
Where the Lunar phases change differently
And the Sun on its path to circumscribe
Often forgets to set for days on end.
The shade of two worlds on the ground is cast,
The one on which my ship is to descend
To shed an earthly drop on it at last.
How small I am below this firmament,
Yet to myself, I appear eminent.

2

Yet to myself, I appear eminent
Beneath the two worlds and a single shade.
And to us, a warm welcome they extend
As our steps fade in foggy cannonades,
"And what is this?" I start to speculate.
To be or not to be, 'tis the question
That, from a vision, makes me hesitate.
My mind looks for a justification
Both for traveling and this adventure
Into the nowhere, into the distance
Above familiar, into space splendor.
I look young again, 'tis my appearance.
Each step I make is the light in the dark.
Every step you take is a lustrous mark.

3

Every step you take is a lustrous mark,
On the other Earth and the other sky.
I watch Eden Birds of a Lovely Spark,
Which makes my heart, in sheer agony, cry
For diving out of the foul world that dies,
For dreaming and singing in its last points,
While, before my eyes, holy doors arise,
And for admiring my soul's enjoyments.
We land at the core of the ancient truth,
As all my companions jump happily.
We fly swiftly toward heaven's mouth,
While all the voyagers cry joyfully.
I see light above the world's settlements,
Over these unreal, blazing firmaments.

4

Over this unreal, blazing firmament,
I realize I am both big and small.
The God of all that is impermanent,
Tortured by pain, always prays to us all
With the help of peace-loving thoughts, He sends
To the ones in a constant state of war,
For delusional humankind that mends
Its fate, escaping the curse of Mors.
"We land into the heaven's mouth," Shakespeare
Says, "And please don't be truly terrified.
Order and peace are crowned as rulers here,
And, by merits, desires are gratified."
As the dawn on this bridge shines and gives peace,
I spot a visage on heavenly sheets.

5

I spot a visage on heavenly sheets;
Then, Shakespeare says, "'Tis an angel of light,
Smiling at the one he joyfully greets.
'Tis the guardian from the home upright
That kept the Maker of the main road safe.
Come to see the bridge, this face of pure truth,
Where every soul on the Earth was once based.
Come, perceive the light of the holy sooth."
I see the angel, my divine brother,
Is the overpass between life and death.
I can see that behind the bright color,
There is a memory of the great strength,
Which reveals the Father's face and its bliss.
I see light from the heart of paradise.

6

I see light from the heart of paradise,
On the border between the void and dream,
I see a lip as bright as melted ice,
That smiles underneath us as a pure gleam.
I take a look left and take a look right,
To find the proper direction in vain;
There is one aspect that both spans and lights
The contrasts in His other domains,
Between plenty of ways and our movements,
Between what's mortal and what's eternal,
Between success and our aspirations,
Between immoral worlds and holy goals.
Being reborn on the celestial sheet,
I discern myself and the word discreet.

7

I discern myself and the word discreet,
On the lip of dark, I find the seraphic light;
I can still see a figure, which is neat
And brings grace to our lives, making them bright.
There aren't any secrets or aches in this world
That originate from human desires
The truths of this sacred domain are hurled
By insight and everything one acquires
Is given by merit while God's kids live
And proceed following a supreme law,
Delightful and soft, which His word can give
While not falling into prosperity's claw
I see the source of life with my own eyes
Stupefied by the glimmer of its guise.

8

Stupefied by the glimmer of its guise
I find the first spirit that feeds the worlds
With the sweet, colorful dream in disguise
And the void offered by the flight through chaos.
In the sea of sin, He sleeps and exists,
Fighting with darkness to create the Earth,
The world sailing into emptiness with mists,
Makes love with the black abyss and gives birth
To great light, getting drunk by its beauty.
The flare porter makes bridges over voids.
To hold lovely Gaia – that's the duty
Of his thoughts that shine over the decoyed.
Now filled with His gleam, I am going Home,
Reflecting myself in the divine foam.

9

Reflecting myself in the divine foam
I am not the same person now; I am
He who eats everything under this dome
Called space, we hear His thoughts sing in our limbs
While a bright world shines from us, we are stars;
There is no difference between darkness
And light when bright thoughts fly, leaving scars
On whole space and making the alliance
That joins shade and glare, giving birth to truth,
Which overcomes gloom by presenting life.
God makes himself by preserving his youth.
And telling what's true by being the knife
Of justice, almost unnoticed, I burn
And even so small, ever bigger, I turn.

10

And even so small, ever bigger I turn,
Being pleased with my own meaninglessness,
Without solving my unresolved concerns,
For our stark reality is doubtless;
In reality, questions are answered
Easily and everything is explained
By existence. What is found, lived, and grasped
Defines us, and the price is dearly paid
In our lives; many thoughts, like atoms, look
For the way to the shiny entity,
With fair scents and pleasant sounds in its book.
The Cosmos screams and cries in gaiety.
Ozar bestows me on his throne to grow –
Admiring my own beloved shadow.

11

Admiring my own beloved shadow,
I do not notice any other truth
And there isn't anything else to be known.
Fully embraced by the enormous strength
Of your hands that come from heaven and hell,
I see the worlds without any lanes out.
The force taken from Hades' many rebels
Lies in the core and exists in the route,
Of omnipotent walk and supreme dreams.
Its luminous whisper goes through the dark
While sleeping above hell and the pearly gates,
Looking like starry rain of hidden arks,
Which dwell in the sky to secure return,
As even myself, I fail to discern.

12

As even myself, I fail to discern,
This looks better to me than the seclusion
From the world where we fall in a pattern,
In which there isn't something called possession,
But everything merges into perfection;
Where the greatest sin is the dissension
From Ozar's fatherhood as deception,
And the whole sphere is Ozar's invention.
The annulment of my own character
Leads me forward to find my deepest core
And purpose; as a faithful explorer
I find the oldest origin and more
Answers; these findings make my mind surprised
Under the blazing fires, space has hurled.

13

Under the blazing fires space has hurled,
This world celebrates itself happily
By making its utopia painted
With sparks in the dark and its harmony
Attained by its creatures, a dark ray floats
Somewhere in the sea, it emits new rays
When the old ones douse; this ray of the wits
Hits the world with its beauty like rain sprays
It pours all the ideas over the void
Which is dry and deserted, manuring
The dark so that the stars, like asteroids,
Could dive to the abyssal depth, finding
Their new home and aim; our steps are sky birds;
I am one with God and one with the worlds.

14

I am one with God and one with the worlds,
Following the stellar traces in dreams
I also become a part of star herds
Before you, I don't chase fairy queens
Or gods; yet, I can see the face, the eyes,
And the lips of the loveliest creature
With which he pours light into the dark skies,
Charmed by the gist of the new disclosure.
Everything floats, lives, dreams, and radiates
Rushing to him and without awareness,
Everything that exists dissociates
With itself in itself, all the brightness
Comes from him at night, chased by my thought spark,
On the spaceship, I'll presently embark.

15

On the spaceship again, I will embark;
And to myself, I appear eminent;
Every step you take is a lustrous mark,
Over this unreal, blazing firmament.
I spot a visage on heavenly sheets,
I see light from the heart of paradise,
I discern myself and the word discreet
Stupefied by the glimmer of its guise,
Reflecting myself in the divine foam,
And even so small, ever bigger I turn –
Admiring my own beloved shadow,
As even myself, I fail to discern
Under the blazing fires, space has hurled –
I am one with God and one with the world.

PLANET ZENA

We landed on planet Zena, where children at the age of ten have more knowledge and intelligence than even the brightest people on Earth, and I want to know what Shakespeare thinks about it.

A DOUBLE SONNET WREATH

1

It is accurate that angels exist
But these are not the angels from stories,
These are the holy creatures that persist
To read our thoughts without difficulties.
These are the higher beings on higher
Levels of development, and not some
Apparitions from books. Like a friar,
I only look back at the distant forms
Of Truth, provided to us by knowledge,
Honesty, the strength of mind and desire,
And the constant vigil over dreams wedged
By the hope of achieving something 'more.'
We perceive, without a precise answer,
That the same rules are valid everywhere.

2

The same rules are valid everywhere,
Even in many other dimensions;
The same consciousness, only with a pair
Of blunders, or more, shines in all sections
Of Cosmos from the core of divine Truth
That we look for even when we don't know,
Even while years run slowly over our youth,
And we strive towards this Gospel bestowed
On us only in dreams; days get faster
And our thoughts, being afraid of time,
Act like something is holding them tighter,
And stopping them from moving, paradigm
Of a life and days that seized to exist
In this reality that yet persists.

3

In this reality that yet persists,
Only movement is important; the truth
That governs our lives and always subsists
Feeds your energy from its distant sooth.
You imagine, expect, flutter, and dream
But only movement is the source of strength;
This planet generates you, and the streams
Of your ideas may flow, but the depth
Of your connection with the world and your
Discoveries make a real-life change
Dive in these beings' truth and open the door
Of the immobile sphere, which can plunge
In another state; this sphere's youth wears
And governs life even in Death's affairs.

4

This governs life even in Death's affairs –
The unborn luminescence of Ozar,
Which, being always new, suddenly shares
Its power from the sky courts and goes far
From there; we go to visit the creatures
That are much more advanced than mortal souls
And are compared only to messengers
Of divinities; they, more than all those
Who live in other realms, build this Cosmos
With their notions and beliefs; their children
Understand more than Earth's experts; their most
Noted feature is their soul; spite doesn't run
Through them, only fondness with acceptance;
There is neither fall nor disappearance.

5

There is neither fall nor disappearance,
Where a conviction is stronger than life.
Before we decide to keep a distance
From this place, try to notice it is rife
With kindness, make an effort to daydream,
To remember your origin in these
Visions, and to see yourself in their stream.
The heaven's bliss will be noticed with ease
On your face, once you recognize who you
Truly are, and you will spot the sacred
Sphere in the unseen light that shines anew,
Beyond the horizon, become naked
Thoughts that give blood to new worlds as vessels;
Thoughts get tangled on their own and wrestle.

6

Thoughts get tangled on their own and wrestle,
In the world that is created to live
Outside the fight for life and death; castles
Of a strange, unknown sea suddenly leave
Their mark on my soul; children float above
The sea, sending me messages with flashes
And calling me to their heights; armed with love
And my dreams, on a white cloud that passes
Across the sea, I start flying toward
Their palace; in my mind, I see the light
So I send them my beam, too; now the Lord
Of this world gives me the holy delight
Of grace, I quest, cured with this contrivance
Against passing and eternal silence.

7

Against passing and eternal silence,
A notion and a beam fight all the time;
Against dark and endless disappearance,
The first spark fights in a battle, combined
With the cloud that brings me to the children.
Neither light nor heavy, almost unseen,
I fly toward the court, where coherence
Of my thoughts was made; although it has been
Unclear where this Cosmos originates
From and lies: it floats above all creatures;
A cloud drifts over us and emanates
Truth so that the world never disappears
In dense shades, when clouds turn rays, like smiths,
Into the dark that they have a bond with.

8

Into the dark that they have a bond with,
Children from another world evoke some
Divine memories, make us trust in myths,
And offer the hope of making dreams come
To pass; strange jets fly up above our heads
Writing their greetings with lovely flashes.
In the new heaven, salvation embeds
Itself and flying gardens with dashes
Of fragrance appear; the children, who aren't
Children, show us the gate, the way toward
Their city; judging by the apparent
Descriptions made by the rays, the award
Of seeing the whole world is our future.
The Universe is the spark and azure.

9

The Universe is the spark and azure,
The Universe is Ozar himself and
His son who beseeches, for this pleasure,
To their union: to shine light with his hand
On countable and countless paths of space
For who knows how many times; numerous
Children grow on these paths, leaving a trace
Of changes on them and making tremendous
Progress of convictions that help them speak,
Fly to different parts of galaxies,
Dream, breathe, and color the world with unique
Shades; the tots go back to the genesis,
Aware of their outset, mysterious
Source of Ozar's sky and great ideas.

10

The source of Ozar's vast sky and grand schemes
Doesn't exist without children, and children
Are everything; they shine brightly and gleam
Like a torch on this road, lit by thoughts that ran
Imperceptible and vivid in their
Unconsciousness; the children we meet know
That; they guide us with mercy and prayers
While we name our eyes for cheating foes,
Finding out that we know almost nothing
And realizing that the birthplace of
Virtue is only modesty, coming
To light with the help of knowledge and love
While being settled on where their flight is planned.
The Universe is life and wisdom land.

11

The Universe is life and wisdom land;
Everything that exists is alive and
Discerns, without awareness, that the hands
Of the world from our dreams shape the soft sand
Which measures time; suddenly, we perceived
A white cloud, or at least something that seemed
Like that, until we went closer, so deceived,
And saw the endless sea that broadly beamed
In the pretty, whitish, delicate foam.
We closed our eyes, blinded by the stunning
Whiteness; in that moment, many unknown
Worlds appeared in front of me, becoming
Clear when Shakespeare stated, "'Tis the fireplace
Which, even in death, warms life and feeds peace."

12

Even in death, the spark of life brings peace,
Which keeps balance with the force that resides
In the depths of its core and in the wits
That won't stop praising life from distant sides
In this world; all children know these statutes
Of our sphere, where skills become instruments,
Not the final goal; kids dream about feats,
Not looking for reasons why detriments
And obstacles exist, but facing these
Threats without any fear, filled with a strong will
And great power that they once seized with ease,
With the help of wit; that's why their time still
Lasts longer, with their days, in all areas.
Angels and we are sublime ideas.

13

Angels and we are sublime ideas
Of the almighty intellect that feeds
Us with itself and never disappears
From our road, but glows gently and succeeds
In defending the star courts of the sphere
Which grows all the time and spins constantly,
Counting acquisitions within the clear,
But unwritten, law; this sphere instantly
Sets new powers in motion when the old
Forces wane; "'tis why we, like angels, are
White," the children announced and consoled
Us "You too are proud creations of stars
That Ozar holds dear. You are fantasies
Uttered in the language of substances."

14

Uttered in the language of substances,
Verities can't be real illusions,
But the entire world of exuberance,
Used for feeding and filling the blankness.
In this way, the energy justifies
Its existence and becomes a lasting
Home for the stars; 'tis how the spark untwines
Itself and the fire continues keeping
The world warm for days; the sphere then starts
Growing on its own while one cleverness
Glows without any directions or expert
Guidance, merging slowly with the bareness
And seeing people like angels who assist.
It is accurate that angels exist.

15

It is accurate that angels exist
And the same rules are valid everywhere
In this reality, which yet persists
And governs life even in Death's affairs.
There is neither hope nor disappearance,
Thoughts get tangled on their own and wrestle
Against passing and eternal silence
In the dark that they have an actual
Bond with; the Universe is the spark, and
Azure of Ozar's sky and great idea;
The Universe is life and wisdom land
Which, even in death, is the area
Of peace; angels and we are ideas
Uttered in the language of substances.

16

Uttered in the language of substances,
Embodied ideas live as God's deeds
In the world of inventive energies
And children, while growing up, make new roads –
There, they find the purpose of existence
Even when wars are openly declared.
While they go around the world with calmness
In their great minds, the children are not scared
Of joining a battle against other
Civilizations since they are also
Adults on their planet, like the older
Grownups there; disobedient and so
Fierce, they know the source of materials.
Angels and we are sublime ideas.

17

Angels and we are sublime ideas
Altogether but, the children of this
Sphere have the truth etched in their memories
As runways for flights over an abyss
Or the warranty of truce, since they still
Haven't lost a single war so far. The tots
Play blissful music in wars so their will
To fight doesn't disappear between the shots
And their spirit stays serene and fearless.
These offspring don't understand the concepts
That slow someone down but remain careless
While turning some problems into prospects
Of fame with their minds; 'tis the stoic art piece
Which, even in death, is the blaze of peace.

18

Even in death, this is the blaze of peace
Because a belief never perishes.
The White Spring constantly flows, without cease,
At the doorstep of Zena and dashes
Into the White Sea; the children's Cosmos
Emperor greeted us at this doorway
And told us, by surprise: "Everyone knows
I am Ozar;" as we saw, Ozar sways
All kingdoms imperceptibly, and these
Children have a vast knowledge of his deeds.
Then, to our astonishment, Ozar seized
And opened a strange box full of many seeds,
Trees, and plants hidden in the new world's sand.
The Universe is life and wisdom land.

19

The Universe is life and wisdom land,
Because existence itself is knowledge.
"Take a look at this world made by my hand,
So that you don't wander through the passages
Of your imagination," said Ozar.
"This little box hides an enormous truth
In its atoms and bits. Listen! These are
The sounds of the music, voices, and youth
Inside the box and they are almost faint,
Yet so intoxicating and quite soft."
Each of the notes reveals the easy gait
Of the course of all lives, and what is oft
Recognized as the crown galleria
Of influence of Ozar's idea.

20

"The sphere of Ozar's sky and idea
Is where we are all one, although we are
Apart; 'tis why my wealth is a real
Possession of yours at the same time; there
Is no hurdle that can't be overcome
By the power of mind and there are no
Forces to stop the sense from finding some
Solutions with its strength because we know
Its quest is for life itself and every
Answer it finds is its food; let the box
Guide you; don't resist; wits and theories
Lead us towards freedom and response.
This world is the gift of grace and glamour.
The Universe is a spark and azure."

21

"The Universe is a spark and azure,
The source of never-ending life and strength,
The Universe is our and Ozar's sphere.
We are all Ozar, coming from the depth
Of his soul to shine and be in this world
At night; 'tis why you should sail the oceans
Of the tiny orb in the box – the curled
Globe of bigger size makes many motions
Inside of them; on this small planet, we
Find the flowers of the greater world
And some great thoughts; once you discern and see
That the laws of pure logic can be turned
Into a maze, you will see the light strength
Of stars that make the dark which they bond with."

22

"The stars dive in the dark that they bond with
So you should dive in there as well to see
How big spheres are made, as in a myth,
Inside smaller worlds, but recall the key
Is to follow the old sound and the path
You walk on; even when you are alone
You are not on your own but in the bath
With all the fragrances of elegance, known
For helping you both fly between stormy
Winds and gain the ancient knowledge that we
Gained as well before making history
With our purity, wisdom, and the sea
Of light in our hearts, marked with defiance
Against passing, dark, and endless silence."

23

"Against passing, dark, and endless silence,
We made history with our innocence
Since there is neither true disappearance,
Despite death nor true loss; your diligence
To remember your descent and perceive
The forgotten colors of our home should
Be kept; note the holy light and believe
In it, because the thoughts that feed you could
Be sleeping at the end of the world viewed
As rootless and the smallest one, jointly
With the sparks of life itself; they live to
Tally your days, which are measured only
By beauty; when thoughts in this world sputter,
They tie and wrestle against each other."

24

"Thoughts tie and wrestle against each other,
Although it looks like they are unaware
Of themselves; what can be manufactured
By the impact of atoms and the war
Between the invisible mind forces
But the beauty of ideas that are
On their way of creating the sources
Of a perfect world and reaching the far
Away goals we dream of; in every heart
Which is alive, there is a belief that
Guides it; look at this box so it can start
Seducing you until you see the cast
Of the whole world and our own existence.
There is neither hope nor disappearance."

25

"There is neither hope nor disappearance,
While grace is hidden in someone's judgments.
Beauty lies in the core of consonance,
Living above time, courses of events,
Truth and hate while soaring in the heavens
With its brightness when darkness tries to shield
It; grace flies in the accord whose essence
Consists of brightness and color, concealed
In the core of our minds, this shiny spark
Is even greater than our intellect.
This sparkle is more vital than the stark
Discipline our wit instills; it affects,
Like the will of God, all thrones and their heirs,
And governs life even in Death's affairs."

26

"Truth governs life even in Death's affair –
The beauty that is the grace, the brilliance
Behind every renascence and the flare
At the rough road's end. Its continuance
Is in this box, visible in many
Wonderful shapes and forms. Fly towards this
Beauty and observe the pure harmony
Of heaven, embrace the wonderful bliss
You feel by perceiving the beauty with
Your look, touch, and sigh. You will see truth lies
And grows in the heart of grace, gaining strength
By consuming the beauty itself. Apprise
The world, with whispers of love that exists
In the reality which yet persists."

27

"In the reality which yet persists,
Above rightness and life, the forever
Lasting light of beauty warms up the mist
Of dark seashores in the midst of nowhere.
As soon as grace commences flying once more,
And our Cosmos wakes up from a long dream,
New roads get created in the azure
Of skies, hope is there again, and it seems
Like people are born anew; the whole world
Is remade in an entirely new form
Which always shifts while being impearled
By wishes and dreams that shine and perform
As ransom for our past wisdom, aware
Of freedom. The same rules are everywhere."

28

"The same ground rules are valid everywhere
And all things are the same in diverse ways,
Every obstacle is only a bare
Deceit; the place we come to is always
The same and the point where we harmonize
Never alters; we manage to detect
Our own pathway every time, and the skies
We appeal to always remain perfect
And immutable; take off and fly, borne
By the wings of the old, divine knowledge
And the older, pure principle; discern
Truth at the door and in the tutelage
Of heaven – our home; beauty's hugs insist –
It is accurate that angels exist."

29

"It is accurate that angels exist,
And everything that can be imagined
Lives as well; both you and the world consist
Of light and were given by it, designed
On the path that remains in the essence
Of time; this path, our world, and hope reveal
Where we should set off, with exuberance,
To reach the end and the birth of real
Existence, which emanates from the same
Place; you listen to the conversations
Of brisk Earth creatures, looking for the flame
That helps you fly; you love these relations,
Unaware they reflect thoughts of importance,
Ancient and said in the sound of substance."

ABOUT THE AUTHOR

Dejan Stojanović was born in Peć in 1959. He graduated from the Law School of the University of Priština. He has published books of poems:

Circling (Krugovanje), Narodna knjiga – Alfa, Belgrade, three editions – 1993, 1998, and 2000.

The Sun Observes Itself (Sunce sebe gleda), NIP Književna reč, Belgrade, 1999.

The Sign and Its Children (Znak i njegova deca), Prosveta, Belgrade, 2000.

The Creator (Tvoritelj), Narodna knjiga, Belgrade, 2000.

The Shape (Oblik), Gramatik, Podgorica, 2000.

The Dance of Time (Ples vremena), Konras, Belgrade, 2007.

Pentalogy: *The World in Nowherness (Svet u nigdini)*:

1. Ozar (Ozar), Udruženje književnika Srbije, Belgrade, 2017.

2. The World and God (Svet i Bog), Udruženje književnika Srbije, Belgrade, 2017.

3. The World in Nowhereness (Svet u nigdini), Udruženje književnika Srbije, 2017.

4. The World and Humans (Svet i ljudi), Udruženje književnika Srbije, Belgrade, 2017.

5. The Home of Light (Dom svetlosti). Udruženje književnika Srbije, Belgrade, 2017.

The Hidden Light (Skrivena svetlost), Čigoja, Belgrade, 2018.

Primordial Spark (Iskra iskona), Albatros plus, Belgrade, 2021.

Centuries and Steps (Vekovi i koraci), Albatros plus, Belgrade, 2023.

Essays:

Creator and Creating (Stvaralac i stvaranje), Albatros plus, Belgrade, 2021.

The New Man and the New World (Novočovek i novosvet), Rad, Belgrade, 2022.

Anthology: *Selected Serbian Plays* (*Izabrane srpske drame*), USA, 2016.

Philosophy: *Absolute*, New Avenue Books, USA, 2024.

A book of his selected interviews, Conversations, was published in 1999 by NIP Književna reč, Belgrade. The Serbian Heritage Foundation and the Association of Writers of Serbia for Intellectual Engagement awarded the book the Rastko Petrović Prize.